MEGA MASH-UP

Cowboys v Trolls
in the Arctic

Nikalas Catlow
Tim Wesson

Draw your own adventure!

nosy crow

Mega Mash-Up: Cowboys v Trolls in the Arctic

Published in the UK in 2013 by Nosy Crow Ltd
The Crow's Nest
10a Lant Street
London, SE1 1QR, UK

ISBN: 978 0 85763 123 7

This book needs **YOU!**

What if some cool Cowboys and some hairy **TROLLS** wanted to be RICH?

What if they went digging for GOLD in the Arctic?
What if the ice started to CRACK and they all **FLOATED OUT TO SEA?**
Would they SINK without trace? Or would they come up with a CUNNING PLAN?
You'll have to finish the illustrations and find out...

Prepare to **LAUGH** while you doodle and SNIGGER while you read.

INTRODUCING the Cowboys of Duff City!

Texas Tom

Lasso Larry

The Sheriff

Hi-Ho Sylvia

Billy Two-Hats

INTRODUCING the TROLLS of Duff City!

Pong

Drudge

Gruff

Bogella

Bonehead

You'll need these...

DRAWING tOOLS

These are the **3** tools that Nikalas and Tim have used to create the artwork in this book.

felt-tip pen or marker

pencil

wax crayon

Using different tools helps create great drawings

PEN

crayon

texture page

pen zigzags

crayon rubbing from lino floor

cross-hatching pencil

crayon rubbing from floor

pencil rubbing from wooden door

scribbly pencil

There are loads of ways you can add texture to your artwork. Here are a few examples

crayon rubbing from wall

pencil dashes

pen circles

DRAWING TIP!
Turn to the back of the book for ideas on stuff you might want to draw in this adventure

Get Ready for a Really sketchy adventure!

Pencils at the Ready...

ON YOUR MARKS...

Let's DRAW!

Chapter 1

The Fools' Gold Rush!

Draw a
snowball
above the Trolls

On a cold, Arctic day, some hairy Trolls are caught in a **bLiZZarD**. "Let's take shelter in that cave," says Gruff, the leader of the pack, brushing snow from his enormous beard.

Add a hungry polar bear

Add some more Trolls

The Trolls huddle together for warmth.
Suddenly, Bonehead holds up a shiny rock.
"**LooK at tHiS**!" He tests it with his teeth.
CRUNCH! "It's GOLD!" he yelps. "Ow!"

Yuk! What have the Trolls been eating?

Draw a Troll lazing in the hammock

The Trolls make plans to build A MINING TOWN. "First things first," says Bogella, Gruff's **Stunning** wife. "We need a hairdressing **Salon** so we can keep our beards looking nice and a **Saloon** so we can spend our riches on crisps and soda pop."

Gruff is thinking about the saloon

Bonehead is dreaming of snow cones covered in slime sauce

But news travels fast, and just as Pong is giving Gruff his first **beard trim**, a bunch of Cowboys turn up. "YEE-HAH!" cries Texas Tom. "We heard there be gold in them there icebergs. We've come to stake our claim!"

What's piled on the wagon?

"We were here first," says Gruff. "This is our town and the gold is ours." The Cowboys laugh. "Call this a town? You ain't even built a mine. Step aside, **fuzz-face**." The Cowboys get to work and in no time at all, they have built Duff City on the ice shelf.

Draw Texas Tom's feet flying out of the swing door

Draw in a flea-bitten old dog

Mining for gold is thirsty work, so the Cowboys and Trolls spend many an evening drinking soda pop in the saloon. Soon, **tempers** start to fray. "What do you mean, my wife ain't no lady?" snarls Gruff, throwing Texas Tom out of the saloon.

Hi-Ho Sylvia runs the town's store. "What you guys need is THIS, the **gold-TECH-Delux-5000 metal-Detector**. It sniffs out gold at 50 paces, but I've only got the one in stock . . ."
"Mine! It's mine!!" cries Bonehead.
"Give it back, you **thieving TROLL!**" snarls Lasso Jack.

Billy sprints back to the **SALOON** with the good news. "THE FELLAS HAVE STRUCK GOLD!!!"

Chapter 2
DUFF CITY ADRIFT

The Trolls and the Cowboys **STAMPEDE** towards the mine.

1.

Fill in the speech bubbles!

2.

Poor old Billy Two-Hats has been trampled underfoot!

The Cowboys and Trolls pile into the rickety lift, the rope starts to fray, then...

3.

4.

SNAP

CRASH! The lift plummets to the ground. The impact causes a CRACK to appear in the ice, which zig-zags quickly across the mine floor. But the Cowboys and Trolls don't notice...

Add a battered stetson

OW

Add a mining cart

The Trolls form a tower and the Cowboys **CLAMBER** up it to reach the surface, hauling the Trolls up after them. Meanwhile, the crack in the ice is spreading rapidly...

Eventually, they all make it back to DUFF CITY.
"Er, guys, we're breaking away from the mainland," says
Bonehead, as the crack in the ice reaches the ice shelf

and cuts right through it.

Finish the crack!

Half the Hairy Hotel is left on the mainland and half travels away with them on the ice shelf. "I guess that means we'll only get half as many customers now," gasps Gruff.

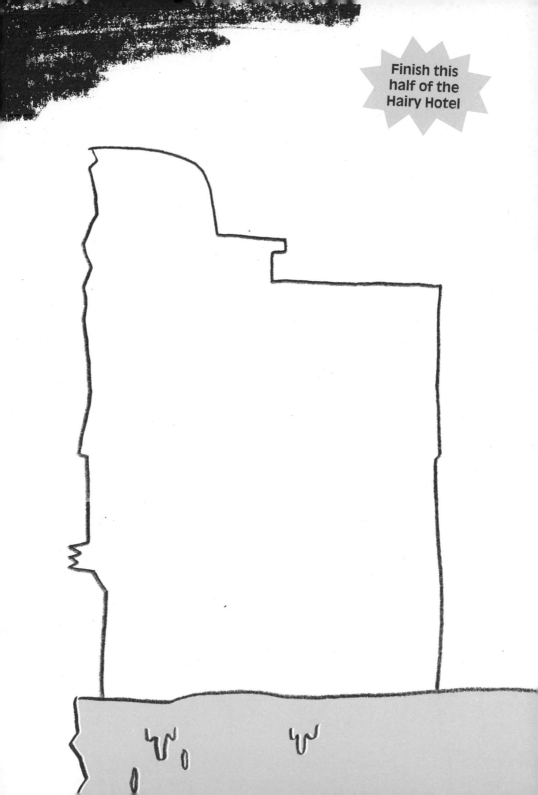

Finish this half of the Hairy Hotel

A fight soon breaks out and the Sheriff does his best to break it up. "Boys!" he cries. "Don't make me throw you all in **JAIL**."

The Sheriff looks round. "Actually," he says, "where IS the jail?" They stare at the jailhouse as it sinks into the sea. The hot sun is **MELTING** the ice shelf, and the shelf is getting smaller, and smaller...

Draw the jail sinking into the water below

Chapter 3
Anything you can build, we can build better!

"We need a plan to get out of here before we're all **fish food**," says the Sheriff. "Think, boys, think!"
The Cowboys frown and stroke their chins.
The Trolls fiddle with their beards and look stumped.

Make the Cowboys look thoughtful

Make the Trolls look confused

"GOT IT!" beams Billy Two-Hats. "We build us a boat and get the **HECK** off this ice! What you got, Trolls?"

Looks like Billy has a good idea

"Well, that was embarrassing!" shudders Pong, while
Billy Two-Hats can't stop laughing.
Just then, a passing seagull **Poos** on Bonehead.
"That gives me a great idea!" cries Pong.

After a frenzy of work, the Cowboys unveil their
PADDLE STEAMER and celebrate by whooping
and shooting wildly
into the air.
**BANG! BANG!
SQUAWK!**

Add a flag

Finish the
paddle
steamer

"Oops," says Hi-Ho Sylvia. "That seagull's had its last poop all right."

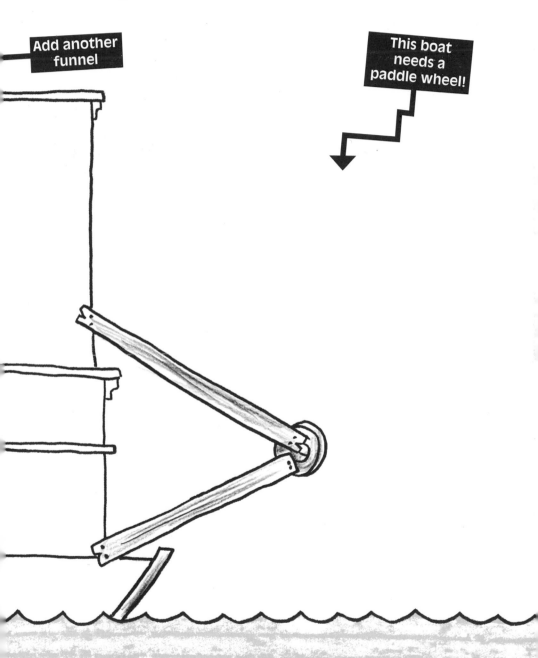

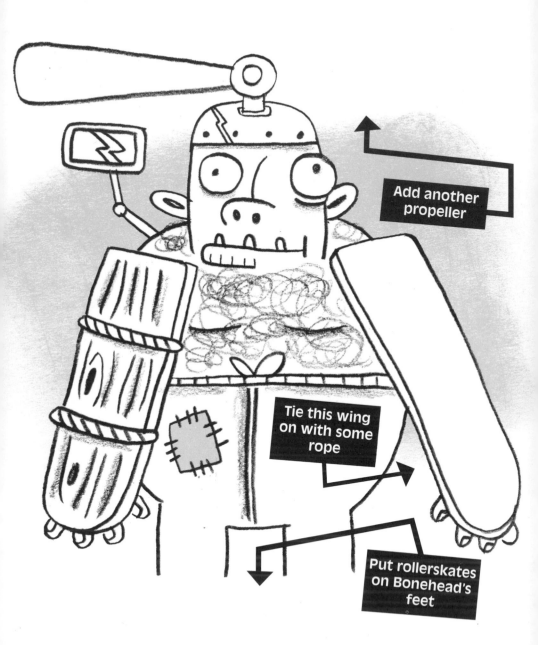

The Trolls have been busy, too. They reveal the Trollicopter, complete with **SNOW RAMP** from which to launch it. "Look and learn, boys, look and learn," nods Grudge, confidently. Bonehead takes a run up, flapping his arms crazily...

Help Grudge build a ramp for the Trollicopter

. . . and crashes straight into the Cowboys' paddle steamer. "You IDIOT!" cries Texas Tom. **"OUR CHANCES OF ESCAPE ARE SCUPPERED!"**

Finish the crash!

Chapter 4
A TROLL IN A BOTTLE

The rumpus wakes a nearby hibernating walrus.
Not best pleased, he starts to **LUMBER** over in
their direction...

The walrus roars in fury.
"H-H-H-He looks pretty m-m-mad!" stammers Billy.
In desperation, Lasso Larry throws a TIN OF BEANS
at it. Followed by a bottle of SODA.
The walrus swallows the lot! **BURRP!**

Throw more
food at the
angry walrus

The walrus quickly drinks another soda, then grabs Bonehead and stuffs him into the empty bottle. "Ha," it says, taking a mighty swing and **throwing** the bottle MILES OUT TO SEA.

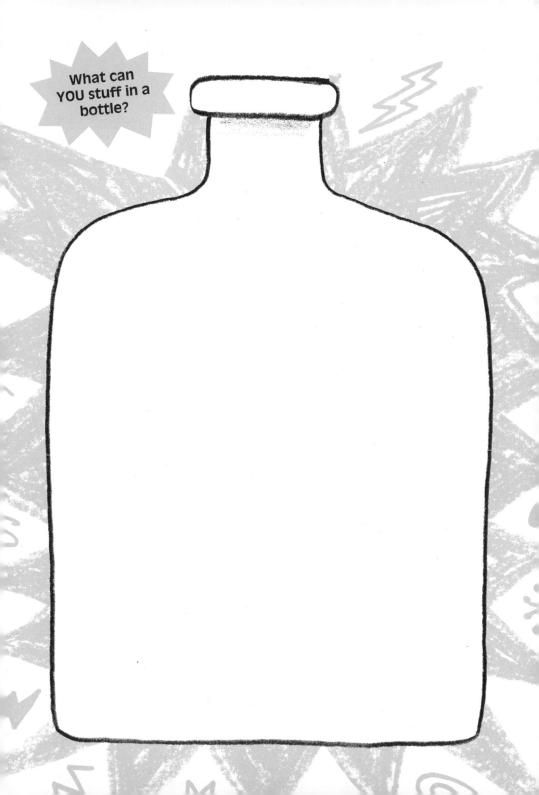

What can YOU stuff in a bottle?

Meanwhile, ONE THOUSAND MILES AWAY on a sun-baked shore, Tony Vegas, the billionaire and theme park owner, is designing the **ROLLER COASTER** of his dreams.

Suddenly, a huge wave crashes on to the shore and something hard bounces off Tony's head!

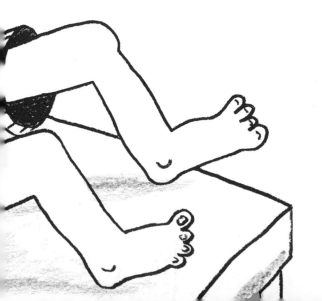

Add a fancy swimming pool

Tony Vegas frees Bonehead from his bottle and listens in AMAZEMENT to his story.

Then Tony has a brilliant idea...
"Come on, Bonehead!" he cries. "**THERE'S NO TIME to waste**! Now, where did I put my speedboat keys?"

OOH! What's Tony found at the back of the drawer?

Chapter 5
If you build it, they will come...

YIKES! Another building has fallen into the water

By now, the ice shelf is tiny.
Everyone is watching nervously as the sharks circle,
GRINNING HUNGRILY. Suddenly they see something
speeding towards them on the horizon...

LOOK! A
meercat in
a dinghy

Tony Vegas swooshes up in his speedboat. "We can't come any closer, or we'll scratch my lovely paintwork," he states. "You'll have to swim across." **THE SHARKS LICK THEIR LIPS.**

YIKES! The water is full of sharks and piranhas!

"Not bloomin' likely!" says Pong. "Trolls, start SHAVING!"
"Sylvia – get **KNitting**!" hollers Billy Two-Hats.
"We're gonna knit ourselves a lasso, hitch it to that
boat and get a super-speedy lift to shore!
YEE-HAW!!!"

We need more
hair! Draw
yourself as a
hairy Troll

Soon Lasso Jack is whirling a large **Lasso** around his head and WHOOPING. Gruff rolls his eyes. "Just get on with it!" he cries. Jack takes his shot and catches the bow of the **SS Billionaire**. "Hold on tight, y'all…"

Draw the lassoed SS Billionaire and mind the paintwork!

Fill the
water with
tiny boats

"WHEEEEEEEEEEE!" cries Billy Two-Hats, clinging on for dear life as the ice shelf is towed back to land. A **flotilla** of boats has gathered to greet them.

Safely on shore, TONY VEGAS shares his vision with the Cowboys and the Trolls. "**AN ARCTIC GOLD RUSH THEME PARK!**" he breathes. "It's going to be Mega!"

OOH! Finish Tony's grand plan

Chapter 6

WALKING IN A WINTER FRONTIER LAND

Arctic-o-matic snow and ice generators are set up on the ice shelf and they begin scooping up sea water, extracting the salt and turning it into snow. The ice shelf grows and grows and soon **CONStRuctioN** of the theme park can begin.

Design an ice generator

Who's watching on the beach?

It's Opening Day and the queue of punters is **Stretching as far as the eye can see**. Business looks set to be booming!

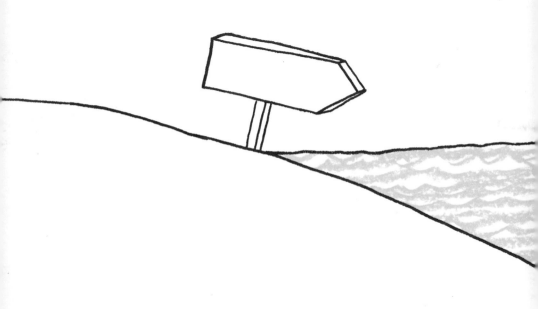

Add an eager queue of customers!

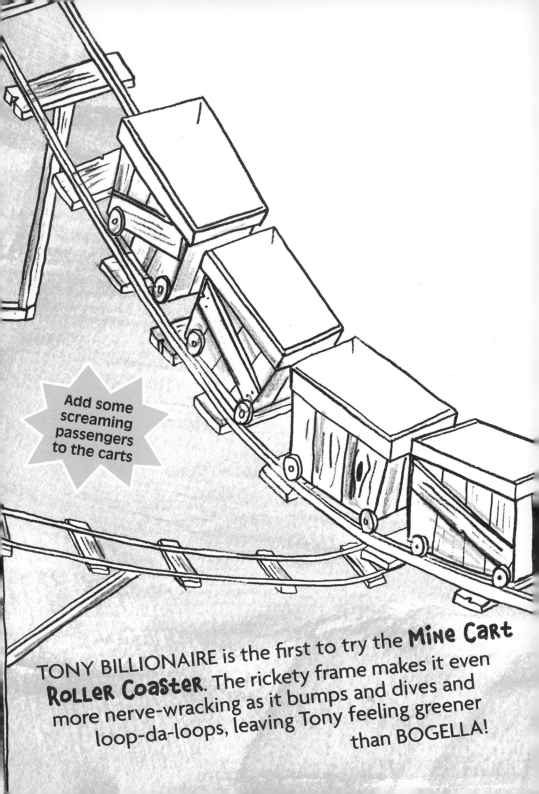

Add some screaming passengers to the carts

TONY BILLIONAIRE is the first to try the **Mine Cart Roller Coaster**. The rickety frame makes it even more nerve-wracking as it bumps and dives and loop-da-loops, leaving Tony feeling greener than BOGELLA!

The Sheriff and Bonehead are selling refreshments and souvenirs. "Get yer ARCTIC GOLD RUSH t-shirt here!" yells the Sheriff. "Print your own design for a fiver!" Mystifyingly, Bonehead's slurpy slug **SLUSHIES** are proving less popular.

Design your own t-shirt

Gruff is working on the Bridge of Trolls and all the punters love his Big Bad Troll act. Apart from a family of nanny goats, who decide to give it a **SweRve**.

Add a nanny goat running away on the bridge

The theme park is a **ROARING SUCCESS**! The Cowboys and the Trolls toast their new-found riches with mugs of hot chocolate and watch the **fireworks**

light up the night sky. "That was one rootin' tootin' adventure all right!" grins Billy Two-Hats. "And all because I thought there was gold in the ice when there wasn't!"

WOW! Create an amazing firework display!

"I got **Stuffed** into a bottle by an angry walrus," remembers Bonehead. "We turned our ice shelf into a theme park," ponders Texas Tom.

"Thanks to Tony Vegas," adds the Sheriff.
"But we never did find any **GOLD**," sighs Gruff.
"Gold?" cries Billy Two-Hats, excitedly. "Where?"

Picture Glossary

If you get stuck or need ideas, then use these pages for reference.

Stagecoach

Things you might see in Duff City

STORE

General Store

Waggon

A Goat on the Run

Products from the General Store

If you like, you can copy the pictures. OR you can draw your own version.

BEANS

SPAM

JAM

DANGER! THIN ICE

A Danger Sign

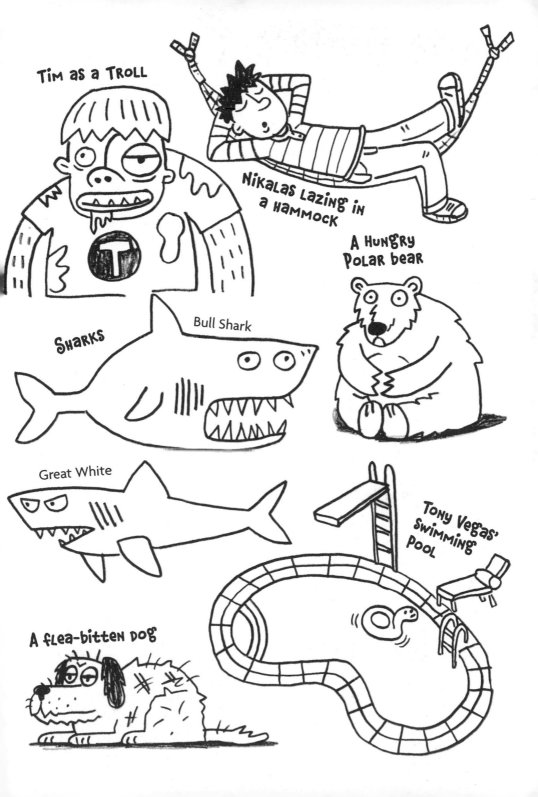

Tim as a TROLL

Nikalas Lazing in a hammock

A HUNGRY Polar bear

Sharks

Bull Shark

Great White

Tony Vegas' swimming Pool

A flea-bitten DOG

Picture Glossary

If you get stuck or need ideas, then use these pages for reference.

Silk underpants

Things in Tony Vegas' drawer

Self portrait

Spare shades

Hair tonic

Gold mirror

blingy ring

Spare comb

CRACK

Sound effects

A TROLL brain

Cowboy snowman

If you like, you can copy the pictures. OR you can draw your own version.

Visit our
AWESOME website
and get involved!

Website →